On *Sesame Street*,
Susan is played by Loretta Long.

Library of Congress Cataloging-in-Publication Data
Hautzig, Deborah. Ernie and Bert's new kitten. (A Sesame Street start-to-read book) SUMMARY: Ernie and Bert adapt to their new kitten as they learn about its feeding and care. [1. Cats—Fiction. 2. Puppets—Fiction] I. Mathieu, Joseph, ill. II. Henson, Jim. III. Children's Television Workshop. IV. Title. V. Series: Sesame Street start-to-read books. PZ7.H2888Er 1990 [E] 89-10583 ISBN 0-679-80420-X (trade); 0-679-90420-4 (lib. bdg.)

Manufactured in the United States of America 1 2 3 4 5 6 7 8 9 10

A Sesame Street Start-to-Read Book™

Ernie and Bert's New Kitten

by Deborah Hautzig

illustrated by Joe Mathieu

Featuring Jim Henson's Sesame Street Muppets

Random House / Children's Television Workshop

It was a big day on Sesame Street.
Susan's cat had four kittens!
Ernie and Bert
came to see them.
"They are very cute!" said Bert.
"Oh, may we have one?" asked Ernie.

"The kittens need
their mother now," said Susan.
"May we take one home
when they are older?" asked Bert.
"Please?" begged Ernie.

"Are you sure you want one?" she asked.
"A kitten is a lot of work.
 You have to feed it
 and clean up after it
 and change the kitty litter..."
Ernie said, "Oh, that's not work.
 That's fun!"

Every day Ernie and Bert
visited the kittens.
Every week the kittens
looked a little bigger.
And every week Ernie and Bert asked,
"Are they big enough
for us to take one?"
Susan always said, "Not yet."
Until one day…

Susan said, "Yes."
Ernie and Bert were so happy!
They already had
everything they needed
to take care of a kitten.

And they knew just which one
they wanted.

Bert picked up the striped one.
"This is my kitten," he said.

"Hey, what about me?" said Ernie.
"He is MY kitten too!"

"Why don't you call him Bernie?"
said Susan.
"BER-NIE, for Bert and Ernie.
Then he will be both of yours!"
Ernie said, "That's a great idea!"

Susan put the kitten
in a cat traveling case.
"Take good care of Bernie!"
she said.
"We will!" said Bert and Ernie,
and they waved good-bye.

Ernie and Bert took turns
carrying the kitten.
"When we get home,
 I will feed Bernie," said Bert.
"Hey, I wanted to feed him!
 What can I do?" said Ernie.

"You can put the kitty litter
in the box," said Bert.
Ernie felt very important.
"Okay, Bert. I can do that."

Bert gave Bernie a dish of cat food
and a bowl of water.
Then he went to find Ernie.

"ERNIEEE!" yelled Bert.
"The kitty litter goes in the BOX,
not on the FLOOR!"
"Gee, I guess I spilled some,"
said Ernie.

Ernie got the broom
and gave it to Bert.
Bert said, "Why should I
clean up your mess?"

Ernie said, "You are the
greatest sweeper in the world!"
"Well, that's true," grumbled Bert.
He swept up the kitty litter.

Ernie and Bert went to the kitchen.

"Oh no!" cried Bert.

There was water and cat food
all over the floor.

Bernie rubbed his head on Bert's leg.

PURRR, went Bernie.

Bert could not help smiling.

"You did not mean to make a mess,
did you, Bernie?" he said.

Then he told Ernie to clean up the mess.

"Why me?" yelled Ernie.

"Because I cleaned up the kitty litter!"
said Bert.

So Ernie mopped the floor.

Bernie chased the mop back and forth.

"A mop is not a toy," Bert told Bernie.

Then he grinned.

"Isn't he cute?" said Bert.

Bernie began to lick himself.

"Hey, Bert. What is Bernie doing?"
asked Ernie.

"That is how cats wash themselves,"
said Bert.

"I am lucky," said Ernie.

"I get to take baths with Rubber Duckie!"

Every morning Bert woke up
with something wet tickling his nose.
"Ernie, wake up! It's your turn
to feed Bernie," Bert said sleepily.
"No, it's your turn!" said Ernie.

"Meow," said the kitten.

"Oh, poor Bernie," said Bert.

"He's hungry," said Ernie.

So Ernie and Bert both got up
to feed Bernie.

Bernie loved to play.

He played with everything!

He played with Ernie's marbles...

and Bert's bottle caps...

and spools of thread.

He jumped up on the shelves
and knocked Bert's paper clips
all over the floor.

One night Ernie was
taking his bath.
"Rubber Duckie, you're so fine,
and I'm lucky that you're mine!"
sang Ernie.
But suddenly Ernie stopped singing.

"BERT!" yelled Ernie.

Bert came running in.

"What's the matter?" he said.

"Look!" cried Ernie.

"Rubber Duckie is sinking!"

Bert took Rubber Duckie
out of the tub.
He looked closely.
"Oh dear," said Bert.
"Bernie chewed a little hole
in Rubber Duckie, old pal."

Ernie was so angry,
he turned bright red.
He jumped out of the tub
and stamped his foot.
"BAD KITTY!" he screamed.
"You ruined Rubber Duckie!
How could you?"

"Bernie didn't mean it," said Bert.
"I don't care!" cried Ernie.
"He ruined Rubber Duckie!"
Bert said, "Don't worry.
We can fix Rubber Duckie."

Bert got some tape and
stuck it over the hole.
Then he put Rubber Duckie
back in the tub.
Rubber Duckie floated!
"There," said Bert.
Ernie was so happy that
he gave Bert a big wet hug.

Bernie purred.

"How come we can never stay mad
at Bernie?" said Bert.

"Because he is just like me!"
said Ernie. "He is cute and funny
and he thinks you are great!"
"Thanks, old buddy," said Bert.
"Anytime, old pal," said Ernie.
"Meow!" said Bernie.